A Note to Parents

Welcome to REAL KIDS READERS, a series of phonics-based books for children who are beginning to read. In the classroom, educators use phonics to teach children how to sound out unfamiliar words, providing a firm foundation for reading skills. At home, you can use REAL KIDS READERS to reinforce and build on that foundation, because the books follow the same basic phonic guidelines that children learn in school.

Of course the best way to help your child become a good reader is to make the experience fun—and REAL KIDS READERS do that, too. With their realistic story lines and lively characters, the books engage children's imaginations. With their clean design and sparkling photographs, they provide picture clues that help new readers decipher the text. The combination is sure to entertain young children and make them truly want to read.

REAL KIDS READERS have been developed at three distinct levels to make it easy for children to read at their own pace.

- LEVEL 1 is for children who are just beginning to read.
- LEVEL 2 is for children who can read with help.
- LEVEL 3 is for children who can read on their own.

A controlled vocabulary provides the framework at each level. Repetition, rhyme, and humor help increase word skills. Because children can understand the words and follow the stories, they quickly develop confidence. They go back to each book again and again, increasing their proficiency and sense of accomplishment, until they're ready to move on to the next level. The result is a rich and rewarding experience that will help them develop a lifelong love of reading.

For Zoë, Theo, and Phoebe
—L. P.

For Richard and Andrel, with appreciation
—D. H.

Special thanks to Garnet Hill, Franconia, NH, for providing Fern's
pajamas and bedding and to Lands' End, Dodgeville, WI, for
providing Sam's sleep-over bedding.

Produced by DWAI / Seventeenth Street Productions, Inc.
Reading Specialist: Virginia Grant Clammer

Library of Congress Cataloging-in-Publication Data
Papademetriou, Lisa.
  Really? / by Lisa Papademetriou ; photographs by Dorothy Handelman.
      p.   cm. — (Real kids readers. Level 3)
  Summary: A young girl is not certain how much of what her new friend says is true and how
much is made up—until she spends the night at her house.
  ISBN 0-7613-2072-5 (lib. bdg.). — ISBN 0-7613-2097-0 (pbk.)
  [1. Friendship—Fiction. 2. Imagination—Fiction. 3. Sleepovers—Fiction.] I. Handelman,
Dorothy, ill. II. Title. III. Series.
PZ7.P1954Re   1999
[E]—dc21   99-12778
                                                                                 CIP
                                                                                 AC

pbk: 10 9 8 7 6 5 4 3 2
lib: 10 9 8 7 6 5 4 3 2 1

Really?

By Lisa Papademetriou

Photographs by Dorothy Handelman

M

The Millbrook Press

Brookfield, Connecticut

My name is Samantha Field. Everyone calls me Sam. I have a new friend. Her name is Fern Pratt, and she just moved here from California. Fern and I have lots of fun at recess, pretending different things.

One time we were pilots, and our plane was about to crash. Another time we were pirates fighting over treasure.

"Prepare to walk the plank!" I said.

"Wait!" Fern said. "I'll show you where I hid the treasure." She drew me a map that looked very real. But I never found any treasure.

Fern likes to draw. Here are two pictures she made. One shows her family. The other shows her old house. That one surprised me. Fern's old house looks an awful lot like the castle at Disneyland.

My Family

Fern Pratt
Superstar
(me!)

Al Pratt
from Italy
makes great pizza!

Fawn Pratt
plays guitar
surfs!

Forest Pratt
a big pain!

My old
house

Fern loves to pretend. Sometimes it's hard to know if she is telling the truth. Once she told me she had a pet deer that lived in the woods behind her house. Another time she said she had a pet snake named Henry that lived in her house.

"Really?" I said. "A snake is a pretty weird pet!"

"Not this one," she said. "Why don't you come for a sleepover on Saturday? Then you can see for yourself."

"Okay," I said. "Sounds like fun."

Saturday afternoon I got ready for the sleepover. I was looking forward to meeting Fern's family. From her drawing, they seemed so cool—except maybe Forest.

I packed my regular stuff. Then I packed a pair of my dad's ski gloves, in case Fern asked me to hold Henry.

When I got to Fern's house, I knocked on the door. A man opened it. "You must be Sam," he said. "I'm Al Pratt, Fern's dad. Come on in."

Mr. Pratt didn't have an accent. And when I thought about it, "Al Pratt" didn't sound like an Italian name. Did that mean Fern only pretended he was from Italy?

"Thanks for having me over," I said.

"Our pleasure," said Mr. Pratt. "Fern told us all about you. It's an honor to meet such a famous athlete!"

"Famous athlete?" I thought. Was Mr. Pratt talking about the winning goal I scored in soccer? Or had Fern made up a story about me?

I was just about to ask when Fern came running into the front hall.

"Hi, Sam!" she said. "Come up to my room!" She grabbed my sleeping bag and pillow, and we went upstairs.

Fern threw open the door to her room. We dropped my stuff on the floor. Then I looked around. There was a small cage by the bed. I peeked inside.

"That's Henry's cage," said Fern.

"It's empty," I said. "Where is he?"

"Nobody knows," Fern said. "He escaped!"

"Really?" I asked.

"Really," Fern said. "Why? Don't you believe me?"

"Uh—sure," I said. But I had my doubts. The cage was empty. Was that because Henry was only a pretend snake?

We played in Fern's room till her dad called us for dinner. Her mom and little brother were already at the table. Fern introduced me to them.

"I'm very glad to meet you," Forest said politely. "Would you like some ice water?"

"Thanks," I said. Forest seemed nice—not a pain at all. I began to wonder if Fern had told the truth about anything.

Just then, Mr. Pratt came in from the kitchen. He was holding two pizzas.

"*Mmm.* Smells good!" I said.

Mrs. Pratt nodded. "Alberto makes the best pizza—just like his mama's."

"My mother is Italian and my father is American," Mr. Pratt explained. "We lived in Italy till I was ten. Then we moved to California. The pizza is Mama's special recipe."

So Fern's dad really was from Italy, and he really did make pizza! I took a slice. Then I unrolled my napkin.

Something black fell onto my pizza.

"A spider!" I screeched.

The spider didn't move. It was a fake!

Fern's brother laughed, and I knew who the joker was.

"Forest, that's not funny," Mrs. Pratt said sternly.

"It's okay," I said. "Usually I love spiders on my pizza—just not today."

I smiled, but Fern was right. Her brother *was* a pain.

After dinner, Fern's mother played guitar for us. Really! Then Fern and I went back to her room.

I looked at Henry's empty cage again. "Henry must be real too," I figured. The thought didn't exactly make me happy.

For a while, Fern and I pretended we were firefighters. Then we were witches casting spells on Fern's stuffed animals.

It was fun!

Soon it was time for bed. Fern and I brushed our teeth and changed into our pajamas. Then I unrolled my sleeping bag—and gave it a good shake.

"What are you doing?" Fern asked.

"Checking for Henry," I said. "I don't want him to scare me in the middle of the night."

"Henry's not scary! He's little and cute," Fern said. "Unlike some other creepy things in this house."

I gulped. "Uh—what do you mean, 'creepy things'?"

"Well," Fern said, "there's a ghost who sometimes walks the hall late at night."

"Really?" I whispered.

Fern nodded. "I've never seen him, but I've heard his footsteps. *Creak, creak!*"

I stared at Fern. "Aren't you scared?"

Fern got into bed. "To tell you the truth, I'm more scared of the wolf."

"The wolf?" I was starting to feel sorry that I'd ever agreed to sleep over.

"Yes," Fern said. "When I see his shadow, I hide under my covers—like this. But I have to say, he never bothers me."

Fern uncovered her face. "Really, the only one who bothers me is the alien."

"The alien!" I said. This was getting to be too weird!

"Don't worry. I'll turn my night-light on," Fern said—as if that would protect us!

"Fern is making all of this up," I told myself. But the stuff about her family had turned out to be true!

Mrs. Pratt came by and flicked off the light. "Sweet dreams," she said.

Fern was asleep in two seconds. I didn't think I'd be able to sleep at all! But soon I started to yawn. Then, just as I closed my eyes, I heard a noise in the hall. *Creak, creak!*

Footsteps! The ghost!

I sat up. My heart was pounding, but I had to see if the ghost was real! I tiptoed to the door. I peeked into the hall . . . and saw Fern's dad.

"Hi, Sam," said Mr. Pratt. "I'm going downstairs for a midnight snack. I hope I didn't wake you."

I let out a big breath. "No, I wasn't asleep yet," I said.

"Well, hop back into bed," he said. "I'll see you in the morning."

I turned back toward my sleeping bag. "So—Fern's dad is the ghost!" I thought. "There's nothing to be afraid of."

Just then, I saw a shadow on the wall. Oh, no! The wolf! Slowly I turned around and saw . . . Fern's stuffed animal.

"You make a very big shadow," I told him. I took him back to my sleeping bag. I did a quick Henry check. Then I snuggled deep inside.

I knew I didn't have to worry about Fern's creepy things anymore. But I *did* wonder who or what the alien would turn out to be. Suddenly I was very sleepy.

I woke the next morning to water splashing on my face. "*Aaack!*" I sputtered. I sat up just in time to see Forest hit Fern with a stream of water.

"You little pest!" Fern yelled. "Get out of my room—and stay out!"

Forest laughed and ran out the door. Fern and I wiped our faces.

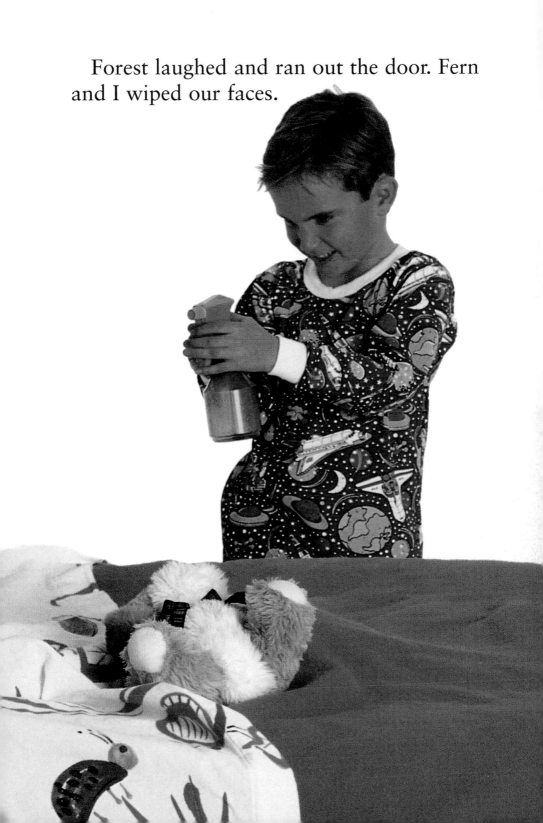

"So Forest must be the alien," I said.

"Well, he sure isn't human!" Fern said. "So he has to come from another planet."

I sat on her bed. "I met your other creepy things too," I told her.

"Really?" she asked.

"Really," I said. "The ghost was your dad looking for a snack. And here's the wolf." I held up her stuffed animal. "Maybe you shouldn't keep him on the shelf next to the night-light."

"I can't believe it!" Fern said.

I couldn't tell if she was serious. "I always thought some of your stories were too good to be true," I told her.

Fern just grinned. Then she hopped out of bed. "Come on," she said. "Let's get some breakfast."

We went downstairs to the kitchen.

"How about monster eyes and toast?" Fern asked.

"What?"I said.

Fern laughed. "Monster eyes. That's what we call fried eggs."

"Uh—I think I'll have cereal," I said.

We sat down to eat. I checked my napkin before I put it on my lap. There were no spiders inside. No snakes, either. I still didn't know if Henry was real or not, but I wasn't taking any chances.

The way I figured it, some of Fern's stories were true. Some were half true. And some were—really—just pretend. The fun part of being friends with Fern would be finding out which was which!

Reading with Your Child

Even though your child is reading more independently now, it is vital that you continue to take part in this important learning experience.

- Try to read with your child at least twenty minutes each day, as part of your regular routine.
- Encourage your child to keep favorite books in one convenient, cozy spot, so you don't waste valuable reading time looking for them.
- Read and familiarize yourself with the Phonic Guidelines on the next pages.
- Praise your young reader. Be the cheerleader, not the teacher. Your enthusiasm and encouragement are key ingredients in your child's success.

What to Do if Your Child Gets Stuck on a Word

- Wait a moment to see if he or she works it out alone.
- Help him or her decode the word phonetically. Say, "Try to sound it out."
- Encourage him or her to use picture clues. Say, "What does the picture show?"
- Encourage him or her to use context clues. Say, "What would make sense?"
- Ask him or her to try again. Say, "Read the sentence again and start the tricky word. Get your mouth ready to say it."
- If your child still doesn't "get" the word, tell him or her what it is. Don't wait for frustration to build.

What to Do if Your Child Makes a Mistake

- If the mistake makes sense, ignore it—unless it is part of a pattern of errors you wish to correct.
- If the mistake doesn't make sense, wait a moment to see if your child corrects it.
- If your child doesn't correct the mistake, ask him or her to try again, either by decoding the word or by using context or picture clues. Say, "Get your mouth ready" or "Make it sound right" or "Make it make sense."
- If your child still doesn't "get" the word, tell him or her what it is. Don't wait for frustration to build.

Phonic Guidelines

Use the following guidelines to help your child read the words in this story.

Short Vowels
When two consonants surround a vowel, the sound of the vowel is usually short. This means you pronounce *a* as in apple, *e* as in egg, *i* as in igloo, *o* as in octopus, and *u* as in umbrella. Words with short vowels include: *bed, big, box, cat, cup, dad, dog, get, hid, hop, hum, jam, kid, mad, met, mom, pen, ran, sad, sit, sun, top.*

R-Controlled Vowels
When a vowel is followed by the letter *r*, its sound is changed by the *r*. Words with *r*-controlled vowels include: *card, curl, dirt, farm, girl, herd, horn, jerk, torn, turn.*

Long Vowel and Silent E
If a word has a vowel followed by a consonant and an *e*, usually the vowel is long and the *e* is silent. Long vowels are pronounced the same way as their alphabet names. Words with a long vowel and silent *e* include: *bake, cute, dive, game, home, kite, mule, page, pole, ride, vote.*

Double Vowels
When two vowels are side by side, usually the first vowel is long and the second vowel is silent. Words with double vowels include: *boat, clean, gray, loaf, meet, neat, paint, pie, play, rain, sleep, tried.*

Diphthongs
Sometimes when two vowels (or a vowel and a consonant) are side by side, they combine to make a diphthong—a sound that is different from long or short vowel sounds. Diphthongs are: *au/aw, ew, oi/oy, ou/ow*. Words with diphthongs include: *auto, brown, claw, flew, found, join, toy.*

Double Consonants
When two identical consonants appear side by side, one of them is silent. Words with double consonants include: *bell, fuss, mess, mitt, puff, tall, yell.*

Consonant Blends
When two or more different consonants are side by side, they usually blend to make a combined sound. Words with consonant blends include: *bent, blob, bride, club, crib, drop, flip, frog, gift, glare, grip, help, jump, mask, most, pink, plane, ring, send, skate, sled, spin, steep, swim, trap, twin.*

Consonant Digraphs

Sometimes when two different consonants are side by side, they make a digraph that represents a single new sound. Consonant digraphs are: *ch, sh, th, wh*. Words with digraphs include: *bath, chest, lunch, sheet, think, whip, wish*.

Silent Consonants

Sometimes, when two different consonants are side by side, one of them is silent. Words with silent consonants include: *back, dumb, knit, knot, lamb, sock, walk, wrap, wreck*.

Sight Words

Sight words are those words that a reader must learn to recognize immediately—by sight—instead of by sounding them out. They occur with high frequency in easy texts. Sight words include: *a, am, an, and, as, at, be, big, but, can, come, do, for, get, give, have, he, her, his, I, in, is, it, just, like, look, make, my, new, no, not, now, old, one, out, play, put, red, run, said, see, she, so, some, soon, that, the, then, there, they, to, too, two, under, up, us, very, want, was, we, went, what, when, where, with, you*.

Exceptions to the "Rules"

Although much of the English language is phonically regular, there are many words that don't follow the above guidelines. For example, a particular combination of letters can represent more than one sound. Double *oo* can represent a long *oo* sound, as in words such as *boot, cool,* and *moon;* or it can represent a short *oo* sound, as in words such as *foot, good,* and *hook*. The letters *ow* can represent a diphthong, as in words such as *brow, fowl,* and *town;* or they can represent a long *o* sound, as in words such as *blow, snow,* and *tow*. Additionally, some high-frequency words such as *some, come, have,* and *said* do not follow the guidelines at all, and *ough* appears in such different-sounding words as *although, enough,* and *thought*.

The phonic guidelines provided in this book are just that—guidelines. They do not cover all the irregularities in our rich and varied language, but are intended to correspond roughly to the phonic lessons taught in the first and second grades. Phonics provides the foundation for learning to read. Repetition, visual clues, context, and sheer experience provide the rest.